Pirate Boy

D1638639

The Barbary Buccaneer

SPARE ANCHOR

HOLD

HATCH DOOR

Barbary Buccaneer

ANCHOR CABLE

ARMOURY

CAPTAIN'S LUXURY
QUARTERS

LAVATORY
LAST FLUSHED
TWO WEEKS AGO

MUSIC ROOM

SHIP'S GALLEY

BILGE

My owners call me
Shut-up-you-silly-parrot
or Shutup, for short.

For Thomas

First published in Great Britain by HarperCollins Publishers Ltd in 2002
First published in paperback by Collins Picture Books in 2003

1 3 5 7 9 10 8 6 4 2
ISBN: 0 00 664776 6

Collins Picture Books is an imprint of the Children's
Division, part of HarperCollins Publishers Ltd.
Text and illustrations copyright © John Wallace 2002

The HarperCollins website address is: www.fireandwater.com

Printed and bound in Singapore

Pirate Boy

Navigated by John Wallace

Yo-ho-ho!

NOT FOR LANDLUBBERS

Collins

An imprint of HarperCollins*Publishers*

Once there was a young boy who had been captured by two evil pirates called Boss and Sidekick.

Day after day the young pirate boy was forced to be their slave aboard the *Barbary Buccaneer.*

One evening the pirates were going
ashore to a party.

"No slacking while we're gone," shouted Boss, the small,
fat one, as they set off for the shore.

"We want this boat spotless when we get back!" sneered
Sidekick, the tall, skinny one.

Pirate Boy just scowled.

As soon as they were out of sight, Pirate Boy turned to his friend, Shutup, the ship's parrot.

"Now's our chance to escape!" he cried.

"Escape!" squawked Shutup.

Pirate Boy seized an axe and...

SMASH!

...chopped through the anchor cable. The *Buccaneer* began to drift silently out to sea.

By morning Pirate Boy had sailed far, far away.

Days passed until...

"Land ahoy!" shouted Pirate Boy.

"Land ahoy! Land ahoy!" squawked Shutup.

"An island!" said Pirate Boy.

"It looks perfect. They'll never find us there."

The shipmates laid anchor and set off for the shore.

"It's paradise!" cried Pirate Boy.
"Paradise!" agreed Shutup.
They'd found the perfect place
for a camp.

As Pirate Boy set to work he thought about Boss and Sidekick.

"Those pirates are bound to come looking for us," he told Shutup. "We must keep watch. And we'd better lay some traps…"

"Lay some traps! Lay some traps!" squawked Shutup.

Then one day...

BOOM!

The pirates were heading straight for the island.

"Time to set the traps!" cried Pirate Boy.

As soon as Boss and Sidekick jumped ashore
they discovered...

...the slippery seaweed trap...

and the prickly cactus trap...

Then there was the biting crab trap...

followed by the bouncing coconut trap!

And then...

the HEAVY, CLANGING WEIGHTS trap!

"I don't like this one bit," said Sidekick, "but mark my words, that boy's here somewhere."

Just then, the island was filled with a terrifying, ghostly sound. The pirates leapt out of their skins.

WOOAAHHH!!

"It's a ghost!"
shrieked Sidekick.

"HELP!"

But Boss wasn't fooled.
"That boy's at the bottom
of this!" he growled.

The pirates searched all over the island without finding Pirate Boy. But they found his camp.

"We'll burn it down and then take back our ship," grinned Boss, nastily.

Overhearing the pirates' plan, Pirate Boy quickly dived into the sea and swam out to the silent *Barbary Buccaneer*.

Pirate Boy climbed the rigging and watched as the pirates followed him to the ship.

Shutup flew below to trick them.

CRASH!

"That boy's down there," hissed Boss. "Go and get him!"

Sidekick started to climb down. "I can't see him," he whispered.

WHHHHOOOOSSSHH!

Suddenly, from high in the air, Pirate Boy swooped down...

POW!

He kicked Boss's bottom and pushed him down the hatch - straight on top of Sidekick!

"Got you!" shouted Pirate Boy, as he slammed the hatch door shut.

The *Barbary Buccaneer* set sail once again.

"It's prison for you two!" laughed Pirate Boy.

"Prison for you! Prison for you!" squawked Shutup.

"Then we'll go back to our island and never be slaves again!" said Pirate Boy.

Don't be too sure, Pirate Boy...

The End

NORTHERN
SEAS

THE WILD NORTH

LAND OF
FIERCE
CREATURES

THE BARBARY BUCCANEER

PIRATE BOY ISLAND

MAGNIFIED X 10

BAY OF TURTLES

THE WESTERN SEA

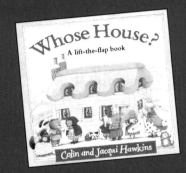

Every child deserves the best...

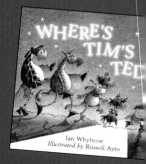

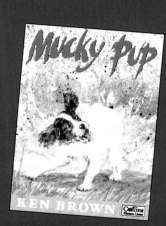

Collins
Picture books

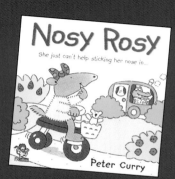